Flotsam and Jetsam

and the Stormy Surprise

For Sarah, Katy and Emily
T. L.

For Dill and Chris
R. R.

First published 2007 by Walker Books Ltd
87 Vauxhall Walk, London SE11 5HJ

This edition published 2014

2 4 6 8 10 9 7 5 3 1

Text © 2007 Tanya Landman
Illustrations © 2007 Ruth Rivers
Cover illustration © 2014 Marta Dlugolecka

The right of Tanya Landman and Ruth Rivers to be identified as author
and illustrator respectively of this work has been asserted by them in
accordance with the Copyright, Designs and Patents Act 1988

This book has been typeset in StempelSchneidler

Printed and bound in Great Britain by Clays Ltd, St Ives plc

British Library Cataloguing in Publication Data:
a catalogue record for this book is available from the British Library

ISBN 978-1-4063-5218-4

www.walker.co.uk

Flotsam and Jetsam

and the Stormy Surprise

TANYA LANDMAN

Illustrated by Ruth Rivers

WALKER
BOOKS

Scan the code to hear Tanya Landman
read the first chapter of this book

One night...

The moon was full, and shining so brightly that it cast shadows of an old man and a young boy across the inky-black waves. They sat – fishing in friendly silence – while the sea licked the timbers of their wooden rowing boat.

In the distance, a tiny beach nestled at the bottom of high cliffs. If the man and boy had looked at it, they might have noticed a small, upturned boat lying on the sand, with an old piece of drainpipe poking out of it. A whisper of smoke

5

curled through it into the night sky, as if a cosy fire was burning inside.

A sudden movement on the sand caught the boy's eye.

"What's that, Grandpa?" he asked.

The old man followed the boy's pointing finger, his eyes creasing as he peered at the moonlit beach. He could just see the outline of a knotted tangle of driftwood and string.

"There's nothing there," he said at last.
"Nothing but flotsam and jetsam."

The boy watched. For a moment, he thought he
saw a glint of silver…

But maybe it was just a trick of the moonlight.
He shrugged, and went back to his fishing.

On the beach a tiny hermit crab was being
taken for a last stroll before bedtime. The
crab scuttled into the waves, his back

glinting silver in the beams of the moon. When he returned from the water, someone reached down and patted him. Then they both turned away and disappeared through a crack in the upturned boat.

On the little beach, nothing moved. Nothing stirred but the sea. Nothing disturbed the silence but the gentle lapping of the waves, and the rise and fall of soft, contented breathing that drifted from the doorway of the boat house.

A heap
of feathers

Flotsam and
Jetsam lived in
an upturned boat
on a tiny beach.
Jetsam's hair was wild and knotted old
string. The top of Flotsam's bald head was
worn as smooth and round as a pebble. Both
had jet-black eyes peering out from brown
driftwood faces. Ropy legs ended in chunky,
toeless feet. Stringy arms bore shapely
hands, with nimble, stick-like fingers.

The tiny beach had been their home ever
since a moonlit night when something had

9

stirred in the inky depths of the sea and they had drifted to the surface. The tide had carried them in and laid them down gently on the soft, welcoming sand.

And every day since then, the sea had brought them some new treasure.

Twice a day the tide went out. Sea anemones drew in their sticky fingers. Limpets sucked down tight on rocks. Crabs scuttled to hide in pools as the water ebbed away. Twice a day the sea returned, flooding rock pools and cooling sun-baked sand. There was a magical moment of high water when the sea paused and seemed to rest for a minute before the tide turned. And it was then that it would lay down a line of strange and wonderful things on Flotsam and Jetsam's little beach.

The sea had brought Flotsam and Jetsam the upturned boat – ripping it from its moorings and hurling it high on the sand one stormy night. It had carried the old piece of drainpipe that they used as a chimney, and the jam jars that made windows as round as a ship's portholes.

Their bed – a sturdy wooden box with the word JA FA painted on the side – had slid from a cargo ship and been washed up on their little beach. They had lined the JA FA bed with dried seaweed and topped it with an old baby's blanket. The sea had given them their biscuit-tin table, their drinks-can chairs, and all the pots and jars that they stored their food in.

The sea had even brought them Sainsbury, a tiny hermit crab who had lost his shell in a spring storm. They hadn't been able to find another shell that fitted him, so Sainsbury now wore a silver thimble which had rolled from the deck of an ocean liner.

The sea could be loud and frightening with its wild storms and terrible rages. But Flotsam and Jetsam knew that whatever its mood, the sea was their friend.

One evening in early spring, a great storm was brewing. It hung in the air, weighing it down and making the little beach feel hot and heavy and uncomfortable.

Flotsam and Jetsam were sitting on the sand, leaning against the boat house watching Sainsbury scamper in and out of the waves.

"'Tis terrible warm," sighed Jetsam. "And damp at the same time. 'Tis hard to breathe proper. 'Tis nasty old weather. Sure as eels is eels. Sure as piddocks is piddocks."

Flotsam was watching the clouds gather on the horizon: clouds that blackened, and grew taller and taller until at last they looked as huge as the cliffs that towered above their little beach.

"I is thinking," said Flotsam, standing up suddenly and grabbing Jetsam's hand. "I thinks a terrible storm is coming. Us must get inside right away."

Whistling for Sainsbury, Flotsam and Jetsam ran for the boat-house door. They made it inside just as the first drops of rain started to fall. Flotsam and Jetsam huddled in their JA FA bed. At the far end of the boat house, Sainsbury buried himself in the sandy toe of the red wellington boot where he slept.

The storm raged and crashed. Flashes of lightning split the sky as they hurled themselves like jagged spears into the waves. The wind howled, the thunder roared and the sea screamed. And then, cutting through the terrible noise of the storm, came the piercing cry of a bird far out at sea – a bird who sounded lonely and afraid.

Sainsbury pulled a clump of seaweed over his head and trembled nervously. Flotsam and Jetsam exchanged an anxious glance and burrowed deep down in their JA FA bed. They could do nothing against the might of the storm. They could only wait for the morning.

When the sun rose, the sea was perfectly calm. Flotsam climbed out of bed and peered through a jam-jar window at the brilliantly blue sky.

"Is it storming?" called Jetsam from beneath the blanket.

"No."

"Is it raining?"

"No."

"Drizzling?"

"No."

"Well, what *is* it doing?" Jetsam threw the blanket aside and sat up.

"'Tis sunning." Flotsam smiled happily. "'Tis sunning good and proper."

In the warmth of the bright spring morning, Flotsam and Jetsam set off to see what had been washed up during the night.

It seemed as if the sea had turned itself inside out. The storm had wrenched strange objects from the depths and strewn them across the sand. There were conches and cowries and shiny green abalones. There were spiky urchins, and delicate pink starfish. There were dazzling white cuttlefish bones, and black mermaids' purses.

And right in the corner of the beach was the strangest thing the sea had ever brought them. A huge heap of bedraggled feathers was piled on the sand.

"'Tis terrible odd," said Jetsam, walking around the heap.

"'Tis most peculiar," agreed Flotsam, scratching his bald head with a stick-like finger.

"What does you think it's *for*?" asked Jetsam. "What can us *do* with it? Us must be able to use it for something or the sea wouldn't have put it there. Sure as jam jars is jam jars. Sure as yoghurt pots is yoghurt pots."

Before Flotsam could answer, Sainsbury scampered up to the heap, took a single feather in one small claw and gave it a curious tug.

In one terrifying movement, the heap of bedraggled feathers erupted and changed into a bird. A very large bird. A very large, very indignant bird. A very large, very indignant bird that towered above Flotsam and Jetsam and looked as if it could swallow poor little Sainsbury in one gulp.

They all stared at the monstrous creature in horror.

But at the very moment the bird stood up on its gigantic webbed feet, it seemed to get dizzy. It swayed to one side, and then swayed to the other. It took two lurching steps towards them and then…

"Look out!" shouted Jetsam. "I thinks 'tis going to—"

The bird collapsed flat on its face, just missing Flotsam and Sainsbury.

"—fall!" Jetsam finished.

The bird lay horribly still on the sand.

There was a long, hushed silence.

At last Jetsam whispered, "'Tis a terrible big bird. Sure as gannets is gannets. Sure as albatrosses is albatrosses."

"But what kind of bird is it?" puzzled Flotsam. "'Tisn't a seagull."

"'Tis not a seagull," agreed Jetsam. "Which is just as well. Seagulls is nasty, bad-tempered things. But suppose that bird there is just as dangerous? What shall us do then?"

Sainsbury's claws clacked together at the thought.

"There, there," soothed Flotsam, patting the little crab gently. "That there bird has got a nice rounded beak. 'Tis blunt at the end, not all sharp like a gull's. 'Tis a beak for dabbling, not pecking. 'Tis a duck, I reckon. A shelduck. I thinks you is safe, Sainsbury."

Sainsbury's beady black eyes blinked nervously. He didn't look at all sure.

"That duck has been battered by the storm. I thinks that bird was what made that noise in the night. 'Tis not a well bird," continued Flotsam. "Not a well bird at all."

"Right," said Jetsam firmly. "Then us shall just have to make it better, shan't us?"

It was no easy task. The shelduck was taller than Flotsam and Jetsam, and a colossal monster as far as Sainsbury was concerned. They couldn't

carry it into the boat house to look after it. Instead, Jetsam fetched the baby's blanket from their JA FA bed and threw it into the air so it landed across the duck's back.

"'Tis terrible chilled, poor thing," said Jetsam. "'Tis proper cold." Not knowing quite what to do next, she sat and rubbed its webbed feet. She felt rather anxious, and couldn't decide if she wanted the duck to open its eyes or keep them shut.

Meanwhile, Flotsam made some food to offer the creature. He fried up some seaweed fritters and spread them with sea pink jelly. Placing them on the lid of a yoghurt pot, he carried them out of the boat house and laid the lid on the sand. Then he fetched a jam jar full of seaweed tea and put it down by the duck's beak.

For several long moments, the duck did nothing. Flotsam and Jetsam watched it anxiously. But, at last, the bird lifted its head, opened its eyes and let out a single, grateful quack. And then it began to eat.

Dipping its red bill into the jar of tea, it dabbled and swallowed until the jar was empty. When Flotsam offered it a piece of seaweed fritter, the duck accepted it graciously, throwing its great head back so that it could swallow.

"'Tis working!" said Jetsam happily. "Us can make it better!"

"Us can," said Flotsam. "And then it can go away, back to where it belongs."

Sainsbury waggled his thimble in agreement.

The duck lay on the little beach all day. When it had been fed its tea – seaweed sausages and milkwort mash – it got to its feet unsteadily. The duck shook the sand off itself and preened its bedraggled feathers until they were smooth once more. Then it looked around.

Sainsbury scurried to hide behind Flotsam's legs.

"It's all right, Sainsbury," said Flotsam gently. "'Tis going now. Us has made it better!"

"I expect you'll be off now," said Jetsam to the duck. "Us is very glad you is feeling better. Goodbye!" She waved.

The duck didn't move.

"You'll want to be off home now, won't you?" said Flotsam. "Farewell!" He waved hopefully.

Still the duck didn't move.

From behind Flotsam's legs, Sainsbury extended a nervous claw and waved desperately at the duck.

At last the bird began to waddle purposefully away. Flotsam and Jetsam and Sainsbury heaved a sigh of relief.

But the duck didn't waddle down to the sea and swim off as they had expected.

Instead, it waddled over to the boat house, lowered its head and disappeared inside.

Sainsbury gave a squeal of dismay.

"No!" cried Jetsam. "You musn't go in there!" She grabbed Flotsam's arm. "Tell it not to, Flotsam! Tell it not to!"

They hurried after the duck, but when they entered the boat house a terrible sight met their eyes.

The duck had climbed into the JA FA bed.

It turned round once, turned round twice, and then settled itself deeply into the dried seaweed with a contented quack.

"That there's our bed!" protested Flotsam.
"You can't get in there!"

But the bird already had, and nothing, it
seemed, could make it get out again.

They asked it politely. They said please
and thank you in all the right places. When
that didn't work they *ordered* it to leave the
boat house. The duck simply shut its eyes,
tucked its head under a wing and went

28

to sleep. They tried to tip it out of the JA FA bed, but the creature was so heavy they couldn't lift even one corner of it. They pulled, they pushed, they heaved and they shoved, but the bird stayed put.

Flotsam and Jetsam had to make a new bed for themselves. They stuffed empty crisp packets full of dried seaweed to make a mattress, which they put next to Sainsbury's wellington boot and covered with the baby's blanket. It wasn't as nice as the JA FA bed, but they didn't have any choice: the duck was there to stay.

And then, feeling rather uneasy about their new guest, Flotsam and Jetsam and Sainsbury sat leaning against the side of their boat house, and listened to the shelduck's soft, contented snoring as they watched the sun sink slowly beneath the waves.

After a moonlit fishing trip, the old man and the young boy left their wooden rowing boat bobbing in the harbour and walked home along the cliff path.

If they had paused for a moment and looked down from the cliffs, they would have seen a little beach with an upturned boat in the middle. An old piece of drainpipe poked up and a whisper of smoke curled out of it, as if a cosy fire was burning inside. If they had looked really hard, they might have noticed a line of webbed footprints that led across the sand and into the boat through a crack in its side.

But they didn't look. They didn't even glance down. To them it was just a little beach, nestling at the bottom of high cliffs: impossible to get to on foot and not worth visiting by boat – too small to bother with.

But it was the whole world to Flotsam and Jetsam and Sainsbury … and a stray shelduck.

The rainbow-coloured umbrel

The duck, nestled comfortably into the dried seaweed of the JA FA bed, slept long and deep and woke feeling totally refreshed. Flotsam and Jetsam, whose seaweed-filled crisp bags had kept sliding out from under them and crackling noisily every time one of them turned over, didn't. When the sun crept over the horizon they were tired and grumpy.

As Flotsam hauled himself stiffly out from under the baby's blanket, the duck gave a loud, happy quack of greeting. It was met

with a moan and a groan and a muttered,
"I suppose you wants some breakfast, then?"

"Quack," the bird replied cheerfully,
snuggling down into the JA FA bed.
It clearly had no intention of moving.

As Flotsam and Jetsam stoked up the fire
they mumbled. As they made the tea they
rumbled. As they fetched the breakfast
things they grumbled.

The duck didn't appear to notice that the
boat-house air was thick with bad temper.
It accepted the jar of tea that Flotsam carried
over to the JA FA bed with a polite quack of
thanks, and then happily started to eat the
yoghurt pot full of sugar kelp flakes that
Jetsam offered.

But poor Sainsbury hated it when Flotsam
and Jetsam were cross. And he was terrified
of the large bird that had made itself so at
home. The little crab hid behind his

wellington boot and
trembled unhappily.

Flotsam thumped
limpet shells of
tea down into
the dents on
the biscuit-tin
table. Jetsam
slammed the tub
of bladderwrack crispies in between them,
making the shells wobble and spilling
hot tea.

They ate their crispies in sulky silence,
and then Flotsam and Jetsam readied
themselves to go gathering treasures.
It looked as if it was going to be a very
grumpy day indeed.

But when they saw what was lying on
their little beach, their bad temper vanished
like mist in bright sunshine.

It was a strange thing, twice as long as Flotsam and Jetsam were tall, and covered in bright, rainbow-striped material. A metal pole protruded from the end, rounded off with a curved wooden handle.

Jetsam walked all around it one way. She turned and walked all around it the other way. She got down on her hands and knees and peered at it. Then she sat down in the sand beside it. "'Tis very nice," she said thoughtfully. "Sure as gobies is gobies. Sure as big blue whales is big blue whales."

"'Tis," agreed Flotsam, nodding.

"But what is it, does you think?" asked Jetsam. "What can us do with such a thing?"

"Could us use it for a blanket?" wondered Flotsam aloud, feeling the thickness of the bright material. "No," he answered himself. "'Tis too thin – and there is all those metal sticks inside."

While Flotsam stood and looked at the new treasure, Sainsbury was scampering up and down the length of it, wagging his thimble excitedly. Just as he reached the handle end, a slight breeze ruffled the material and lifted an edge off the sand. Sainsbury's beady black eyes widened, and he dashed inside.

"Sainsbury! Come out of there!" called Jetsam. But Sainsbury was scuttling all the way to the end; they could see the outline of his thimble against the material. When he got there, he couldn't – or wouldn't – come out.

"He's stuck!" Jetsam said, pushing Flotsam towards the treasure. "Go and rescue him! Off you goes."

Flotsam dropped to his knees, lifted the edge of the material and crawled slowly inside. But he was bigger than Sainsbury, and as he edged forward something extraordinary happened.

To his surprise, the metal sticks inside started to slide, and move, and as he went further and further along the central pole he could see the structure expand and begin to open.

"'Tis amazing!" gasped Flotsam. "'Tis proper wonderful!" He followed Sainsbury right up to the end and crouched there, looking back at Jetsam, who was still sitting on the sand.

"'Tis marvellous!" cried Flotsam. "Come on inside!"

"'Tis marvellous, yes," replied Jetsam. "But is it safe?"

Just then there was a loud ping! and the entire thing collapsed, trapping Sainsbury and Flotsam inside.

PING!

Flotsam gave a muffled shout of surprise and wriggled around, trying to find the way out.

Jetsam had noticed something. There was a sliding ring on the pole from which all the metal sticks seemed to sprout. Suppose she pushed the ring up to the top?

Jetsam crawled under the material, clasped the ring and started to push. She pushed and she shoved and she slid the ring further and further up the pole, and as she did so the thing widened and opened like a blossoming flower. When she reached Flotsam and Sainsbury, there was a loud click as the catch at the top flicked into position.

There it was – circular, brightly coloured and big enough for Flotsam, Jetsam and Sainsbury to sit in.

"What is it?" whispered Flotsam in wonder.

Jetsam had noticed the writing on the pole. The sea had worn some of the letters away, but there were enough for her to read. "I knows what it is," she said confidently. "'Tis an umbrel. That's what it is."

Flotsam nodded with satisfaction.

"I wonders what us can do with it?"

He cupped his bald head in his stick-like fingers and said quietly, "I is thinking."

Jetsam knew that the thoughts that Flotsam thunk were good ones, so she didn't disturb him. For a long time, they all simply sat on the sand in the umbrel and did nothing.

But then Flotsam stood up and took a long look at the biggest rock pool on their beach. He looked at the umbrel. And then he said, "I've thunk."

Flotsam put the umbrel carefully on the water. "It floats!" he said. "I thunked it would."

"It floats," echoed Jetsam. "But what does us do with a treasure that floats?"

Flotsam smiled happily. "Us gets in," he said. "Us goes for a little trip." He stepped off the rock he was standing on into the

umbrel. It flipped over. Flotsam landed on
his bottom in the shallow water.

Jetsam giggled.

"It will work,"
grumbled Flotsam, setting the umbrel
upright once more. "Us just needs to do
it proper."

"How?" asked Jetsam. "It'll tip over again
if us gets in."

"No it won't," said Flotsam firmly. "Us must do it together. Us must get right in the middle. One each side of the pole, see?"

"How does us do that?"

"Us jumps."

"Jumps?" Jetsam turned a little pale.

"Jumps!" said Flotsam firmly. "NOW!" And, grasping Jetsam tightly with one hand and clutching Sainsbury's claw with the other, Flotsam leapt into the centre of the umbrel.

It wobbled, it bobbed, it rocked from side to side, but it didn't tip over. The force of their jump sent the umbrel twirling gracefully across the water until it slowed and came to rest right in the middle of the rock pool.

Carefully, steadily, Flotsam and Jetsam crept towards opposite sides. They peered over the edge and looked straight down into the deep, clear water.

"Oh!" gasped Jetsam. "'Tis proper marvellous! Sure as dolphins is dolphins, sure as mermaids is mermaids."

"Ah," agreed Flotsam. "'Tis nice to be *on* the water, and not *next* to it. 'Tis proper lovely."

Sainsbury was so little that he could scamper from side to side without rocking the umbrel. He ran between Flotsam and Jetsam, peering over the edge at each new wonder. Sea anemones waved their tentacles lazily. Shrimps raced busily between clumps of seaweed. Periwinkles crawled over rocks, leaving broad trails behind them. Silver fishes darted here and there. Mussels sucked water through their open shells.

Flotsam and Jetsam and Sainsbury gazed into the deep water for a very long time. But at last it was time for tea.

"Us must go home," sighed Jetsam. "I expect that there duck will want to eat. Sure as seaweed sausages is seaweed sausages. Sure as milkwort mash is milkwort mash."

At the mention of the duck, Sainsbury blinked nervously.

"You doesn't like it, does you?" said Flotsam. "Poor little Sainsbury."

Thinking of the duck in their nice cosy JA FA bed made Flotsam and Jetsam sink into a gloomy silence.

A warm breeze ruffled the surface of the pool and pushed the umbrel back to the side.

Getting out was trickier than getting in. The umbrel rocked as Jetsam and Sainsbury climbed out, and when Flotsam stood up, it tipped him into the shallow end of the rock pool. But soon they were all standing safely on the side. Flotsam, dripping slightly, took the umbrel's handle and heaved it out of the water.

Suddenly a gust of wind filled the dome of bright material and the umbrel was lifted into the air. Flotsam gave a cry of panic as his feet left the ground.

"Help!" he screamed as he was blown towards the sea.

With a shriek of alarm, Jetsam ran after him.

"I is coming! I is coming, Flotsam!"

With a gigantic leap off the rocks, she grabbed one of Flotsam's toeless feet. But then – to her horror – Jetsam too was lifted into the air. Sainsbury sprang after her. He seized her ropy leg in his pincer claws.

"Ow! Ow! OW!!!" she shrieked. "That hurts! Let go! Let go, Sainsbury!"

Ow!

The gust of wind dropped
as suddenly as it had risen, and
Flotsam, Jetsam and Sainsbury landed
in a tangled heap in the soft sand beside
the boat house. The dome of the umbrel
came down on top of them, almost covering
them completely.

"Us must get this thing folded and
put away," gasped Flotsam. "'Tis proper
dangerous."

"No, 'tisn't," said Jetsam. She was lying
on her back, looking up at the domed roof.
"I has had a thunk! I is thinking it will keep
the rain off this way up. Can you see what
us has? 'Tis a new house! A summer house!
Us can stay out here until that duck goes.
Sainsbury will be much happier out here,
won't you, Sainsbury?"

The little crab waggled his thimble in
agreement.

Flotsam and Jetsam and Sainsbury crawled out of the umbrel. The curved handle had sunk into the soft sand and Flotsam and Jetsam pushed it down further until the umbrel was well wedged. The spokes at one side dug into the sand like tent pegs, and Flotsam and Jetsam weighed the edge of the material down with pebbles so that it wouldn't blow away again.

While Flotsam gave the duck a pot of kelp flakes for its tea, and fetched the baby's blanket, Jetsam scraped a square hole in the sand and filled it with enough dried seaweed to make a comfortable bed. Together they dragged Sainsbury's red wellington boot from the boat house and tucked it against the rainbow-coloured wall of the umbrel.

They lit a campfire on the beach, and had a barbecue of bladderwrack burgers and sea lettuce.

And then, feeling very happy, Flotsam and Jetsam and Sainsbury sat leaning against the side of the umbrel, and listened to the shelduck's soft, contented snoring as they watched the sun sink slowly beneath the waves.

The old man and the young boy walked across the cliffs every day, down to the small harbour where the wooden rowing boat bobbed up and down. If the water was calm, the old man would row out to sea. There they would sit, fishing together in friendly silence, while the waves lapped and slapped against the boat's timbers.

If they had paused for a moment and looked down from the cliff path, they would have seen a little beach with an upturned boat in the middle. A brightly-coloured umbrella was beside the boat, its handle wedged into the sand as if some small

53

*person was using it as a tent. If they had looked
really hard, they might have noticed a charred
spot near by where someone had lit a barbecue.*

*But they didn't look. They didn't even glance
down. To them it was just a little beach, nestling
at the bottom of high cliffs: impossible to get to on
foot and not worth visiting by boat – too small to
bother with.*

*But it was the whole world to Flotsam and
Jetsam and Sainsbury … and a stray shelduck.*

The wheel

The first rays of the rising sun filtered through the umbrel's fabric and flooded it with glorious, rainbow-coloured light. Flotsam and Jetsam woke and looked around in wonder. In the timbered boat house, the sun had to creep and trickle its way in through jam-jar windows and down the drainpipe chimney. But now they lay bathed in bright sunshine.

"'Tis sunning!" exclaimed Flotsam, throwing back the baby's blanket.

"'Tis sunning good and proper!" agreed Jetsam.

Sainsbury started scampering around in excited little circles.

Flotsam lit a fire on the sand, and put on a tin of water to boil.

The crisp morning air was clear and fresh, and filled with the promise of a warm day to come. Rays of sunlight slanted across the sea, catching the tops of the waves and colouring them a brilliant turquoise. The sea pinks and wild thyme that dotted the cliffs and spilt down onto the rocks were at their prettiest. Flotsam and Jetsam thought that their little beach had never looked more beautiful.

When Flotsam had made tea, Jetsam carried a jar full into the boat house for the duck, who quacked a friendly greeting. The bird was looking quite well, but showed no sign at all of wanting to leave. Just as soon as it had been given its breakfast, it dug itself deeper than ever into the JA FA bed. And on that particular morning neither

Flotsam nor Jetsam nor Sainsbury minded at all. The umbrel was a wonderful tent, and they all felt as though they were on holiday.

The sea had reached the magical moment of high water, when it seemed to pause, and rest awhile before turning and ebbing away.

Flotsam and Jetsam sat on the sand, munching bladderwrack crispies – which seemed to be crunchier and even more delicious now they were being eaten outdoors.

When they had finished breakfast, the tide turned. The sea began to ease its way back down the beach, one wave at a time, leaving something strange and wonderful on the sand for Flotsam and Jetsam.

Sainsbury spotted it first, and scampered over to examine the object which was half buried in the sand. He let out an excited little squeal, and Flotsam looked across at him.

"What has you found, Sainsbury?" he asked,

walking over to where the crab was bouncing up and down with excitement.

Jetsam joined them, and together they scraped the sand away until their new treasure was revealed.

It was the wheel from a child's bicycle, still attached to a section of broken, rusty frame. Jetsam regarded it with a puzzled frown. But Flotsam looked at the wheel with an expression of rapt wonder.

"'Tis marvellous!" he gasped. "'Tis quite astonishing!"

"It is?" asked Jetsam.

"Yes. 'Tis," replied Flotsam firmly. "'Tis a wondrous treasure."

"Is you sure?" said Jetsam. "What does it do?"

"I'll show you," promised Flotsam, taking hold of the frame and dragging the wheel across the sand. "It will be proper amazing. Just you wait and see."

Jetsam built a sandcastle with Sainsbury
and they paddled in the rock pools. Then
she made a marvellous picnic lunch of
seaweed sausage rolls and samphire tarts,
but Flotsam was too busy to come and eat
it. He spent the entire morning in the cave
at the foot of the cliffs where he and Jetsam
stored their treasures.

All day Flotsam banged and crashed,
fiddled and tinkered, bent and stretched.

Eventually he heaved such a massive sigh
of contentment that Jetsam heard it from
the other end of the beach.

"Has you finished?" she asked,
approaching the mouth of the cave.
Sainsbury scuttled over eagerly.

"Yes, I has," announced Flotsam proudly.

He emerged into the sunlight,
pushing his invention
before him.

The wheel and its
rusty bit of bicycle
frame were now fixed
to a wooden box
with lengths of
wire.

Flotsam had fastened the planks from a blown-down fence onto the top of the box with string. They made a pair of long handles.

Jetsam blinked twice and then said politely, "'Tis lovely. 'Tis proper marvellous. Sure as clams is clams. Sure as limpets is limpets."

Flotsam smiled broadly.

But then Jetsam asked, "What is it?" and Flotsam's smile slipped a little.

He tapped the box, pointing to the worn lettering on the side. "'Tis obvious what it is," he said crossly. "'Tis a samtea."

"Ah…" said Jetsam, slowly nodding. "But what's it for?"

"Us puts things in it. Treasures the sea brings. Us puts them all in here and then takes them over to the cave, see? Us needn't spend all day gathering, then. No more of all that backwards and forwards, backwards and forwards. Us can do it all in one go. 'Twill be quicker. Us has transport!"

Flotsam started to push the samtea ahead
of him towards the line of treasures that the
sea had left at high tide. But he hadn't gone
far before the wheel got stuck in the soft
sand.

Flotsam reversed crossly, dragging the
wheel free and then setting off once more.
The same thing happened again. He pulled
the wheel clear and decided to walk
backwards instead. This way he managed
to reach the damp sand that had been
firmed and flattened by the sea.

Here it was easier. Flotsam could push the samtea ahead of him, throwing fishing floats and pieces of driftwood and shells and bits of net into it. He walked along the line of treasures, throwing everything into the samtea until it was piled high.

And then he had a problem. How was he going to drag it back to the cave?

Jetsam helped, and they took a handle each. Everything was fine until they reached the soft sand near the cave mouth. Here the wheel sank, the box tipped sideways and the samtea overturned, spilling all their treasures onto the beach. The rusty bicycle frame gave a grating sigh and collapsed. There was a snap and a crack, and the wheel broke loose.

"Didn't work!" said Flotsam crossly. "All day that took me! And now 'tis gone and broke!"

He sat down, cupped his bald head in his stick-like fingers and sulked.

Jetsam patted him on the shoulder absent-mindedly. She was watching the wheel, which was lying on its side.

Without a word, she went into the cave. There in the far corner lay a small piece of old lino. It had once been a floor tile, but was so ancient and battered that its edges had worn off. It was now almost perfectly circular, with a small hole right in the middle. Jetsam carried it out of the cave and put it down on top of the wheel.

Then she picked up the whole thing and placed it on top of the wooden box so the wheel was lying flat. The axle running through the centre of the wheel slotted neatly into a hole in the wood. She gave the wheel a push. It spun freely.

Jetsam climbed up and sat down on the wheel, one leg hanging over its rim. She pushed against the box with her foot.

Flotsam was too busy sulking to notice what she was doing. It wasn't until she gave a delighted giggle that Flotsam looked up.

Jetsam was spinning, whizzing around and around at high speed, chuckling to herself. Sticking a foot out to slow herself down, she called, "'Tis proper marvellous. Sure as twirling is twirling. Sure as whirling is whirling. Come on, Flotsam. You have a go."

Flotsam was still upset about the failure of his samtea, but the spinning wheel looked like too much fun for him to carry on sulking. He sat on the edge, pushing himself around and around with one foot, giggling happily. And then he noticed Sainsbury.

The little crab was watching, his thimble quivering with excitement.

"You is right," said Flotsam. "'Tis your turn, Sainsbury."

Sainsbury's legs were too short for him to propel himself around and around. Lifting the crab into the centre of the lino, Flotsam and Jetsam gave the wheel a good, hard spin.

Too hard.

Sainsbury was thrown clean off the wheel, up into the air. Flotsam and Jetsam watched in horror as the crab flew across the beach,

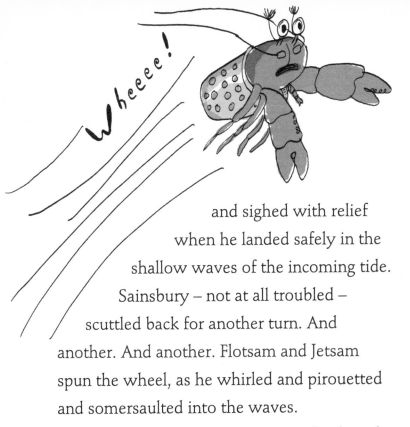

Wheeee!

and sighed with relief
when he landed safely in the
shallow waves of the incoming tide.
Sainsbury – not at all troubled –
scuttled back for another turn. And
another. And another. Flotsam and Jetsam
spun the wheel, as he whirled and pirouetted
and somersaulted into the waves.

They played with the spinning wheel until
the sun started to go down.

And then, feeling nicely dizzy, and weak
from so much giggling, Flotsam and Jetsam
and Sainsbury sat leaning against the side of
the umbrel, and listened to the shelduck's soft,
contented snoring as they watched the sun
sink slowly beneath the waves.

After a peaceful fishing trip, the old man and the young boy walked along the cliff path that led homewards.

If they had paused for a moment and looked down from the cliffs, they would have seen a little beach with an upturned boat in the middle, and a rainbow-striped umbrella beside it. If they had looked really hard, they might have noticed a child's bicycle wheel lying flat, covered with a disc of lino as if some small person had turned it into a roundabout.

But they didn't look. They didn't even glance down. To them it was just a little beach, nestling at the bottom of high cliffs: impossible to get to on foot and not worth visiting by boat – too small to bother with.

But it was the whole world to Flotsam and Jetsam and Sainsbury … and a stray shelduck.

The whoosh

As long as the weather stayed warm and dry, Flotsam and Jetsam were very happy camping in the umbrel. But one night it started to rain. There was no thunder. No lightning. No howling wind. Just the steady *drip-drip-drip* of heavy rain. Rain poured down the sides of the umbrel and streamed through the open door. Rain seeped under the edges, and trickled into Flotsam and Jetsam's dug-out bed. Rain carved out little curving paths across the floor, until it felt to Flotsam and

Jetsam as though they were sleeping in the middle of a river.

When they woke in the morning, the rain had slowed to a misty drizzle. Sainsbury climbed out of his wellington boot quite happily – he didn't mind the wet at all. But Flotsam and Jetsam were cold and stiff and grumpy.

The wood for the campfire was damp. After a long time Flotsam managed to light it, but it smoked and smouldered horribly, and gave off so little heat that the can of water he'd put on wouldn't boil. They had to drink tepid tea, which did nothing to cheer them up, and their breakfast crispies were so soggy that neither Flotsam nor Jetsam could bear to eat them.

Instead, Jetsam took them inside for the shelduck – who didn't seem to mind what it ate as long as it was given breakfast in bed.

Jetsam collected two crisp packets from the boat house. These were their waterproof Walkers, and were handy for keeping out the worst of the wet.

Flotsam and Jetsam pulled their Walkers on over their heads, and set off to gather treasures.

There were bits of coloured string and tangles of netting; twisted twigs of driftwood and smooth planks; fragments of broken glass that had been worn as smooth as pebbles in the restless waves.

And there, lying on the sloping sand at one side of the boat house, was a long sheet of plastic.

"Now that will be proper useful," said Jetsam. "Sure as tins is tins. Sure as boxes is boxes."

"It will," agreed Flotsam. "Us could put that over the umbrel and it would keep us proper dry. But 'tis too big to manage like that." He sat for a moment, cupping his bald head in his stick-like fingers. "I thinks us should fold it," he said. "That's the thing to do."

"Shall us start at the top?" asked Jetsam.

Without waiting for an answer, she climbed to the top of the slope, and Flotsam followed.

Jetsam bent down to grab a corner of the plastic sheet, but as she leant forward, she stepped onto the plastic.

The wet, slippery plastic.

"Waaooh!!"

Jetsam's feet shot out from under her. She thudded backwards onto her bottom, spun round, flopped onto her side and

then whooshed down the entire length of
the sheet. When she landed
in the soft sand, Jetsam
sat up, blinked twice in
surprise, and stood back up.

"I went whoosh!" she said indignantly, rubbing her sore bottom. "That there thing made me go whoosh! 'Tis dangerous!"

"'Tis all right," called Flotsam from the top of the slope. "'Tis perfectly safe so long as you're— *Waaoooh!!*"

Flotsam whooshed down the plastic and crashed into the sand beside Jetsam.

"I told you," said Jetsam crossly. "'Tis a whoosh. 'Tisn't safe."

Flotsam stood up. "'Tis all right," he said again. "Us just needs to find a way to fold it without stepping on it. I'm sure us shall manage."

He was wrong. Try as they might, Flotsam and Jetsam couldn't seem to find a way of rolling up the whoosh. It was vast and unmanageable, and as slippery as a gigantic bar of soap. Neither of them could get a proper grip on it, and every time one of them accidentally set foot on the plastic

they slipped over.
Flotsam and Jetsam
began to feel as if the
whoosh was alive.
It seemed to be
teasing them.

They approached it from opposite sides.

"*Waaoooh!!*"

They approached
it from the bottom.

"*Waaoooh!!*"

They approached it diagonally.

"*Waaoooh!!*"

They tried crawling up to it on their hands
and knees. They tried edging up to it on their
bottoms. They even tried sneaking up to
it by wriggling along on
their tummies.

"*Waaoooh!!*"

"*Waaoooh!!*"

Nothing worked.

Flotsam and Jetsam climbed up the slope and looked at the plastic in despair. They rubbed their bruises as they watched the sea edging its way back up the beach, wave by wave, and stretching out wet fingers towards the bottom edge of the whoosh.

"Us can't do it," sighed Flotsam. "Us shall just have to leave it there."

"Us shall," agreed Jetsam.

And then there was a very strange sound from the boat house.

The shelduck was quacking. Quacking loudly with tremendous excitement. Quacking with pride and delight. And in between the quacks there was a new noise – something Flotsam and Jetsam had never heard before. A soft, high-pitched peeping.

Flotsam and Jetsam looked at each other in astonishment. Sainsbury scurried nervously to hide behind their legs.

"What's going on?" asked Jetsam.

"Should us go and look?" wondered Flotsam.

Before either of them could move towards the boat house, there was a commotion from within and suddenly the shelduck was standing in the doorway quacking at the top of its voice.

"It's out!" cried Jetsam, clasping Flotsam's hand. "It's better at last! Us has made it well again!"

"I think us has done more than that," whispered Flotsam in astonishment. "Look!"

The shelduck was waddling towards them up the slope, its eyes gleaming brightly with happiness. And several paces behind waddled a tiny, fluffy duckling.

Jetsam's mouth fell open. She tried to speak, but all that came out was a small, astounded squeak. Her eyes widened. She raised a finger and pointed at the boat-house door. Another duckling emerged …

followed by another …

and another …

and another.

Flotsam and Jetsam watched as one by one a line of eleven fluffy ducklings waddled up to join their mother. Their high-pitched peeping filled the air.

The shelduck looked at Flotsam and Jetsam, and gave a soft, grateful quack. She lowered her great head and Jetsam patted it gingerly.

"Well, no wonder you didn't want to go! I never knew you had laid eggs in our JA FA bed. Who'd have thunk it!"

"I expect you really is going now, isn't you?" said Flotsam.

They couldn't help feeling a little sad, until Sainsbury gave a squeal and reminded them that he would be very relieved to see the duck leaving at last. Especially as the eleven fluffy ducklings were looking at him with their bright, inquisitive eyes. One of them even attempted a curious peck at his silver thimble.

Flotsam scooped Sainsbury up into his arms, out of their reach.

The duck raised her head once more. And then, taking a deliberate step forward, she launched herself gracefully onto the whoosh and slid into the waves as stately and dignified as an ocean liner.

One by one each of the ducklings followed – with a lot less grace and a lot more muddle

than their mother. Some slid sideways. Two slid backwards and crashed, bottom first, into the sea. One tripped at the top and slid the length of the whoosh upside down, its little webbed feet thrashing helplessly in the air. When it hit the waves it disappeared for a moment in the foam, and Jetsam grasped Flotsam's arm anxiously. But the little bird righted itself magically and, peeping, lined up behind its brothers and sisters.

Soon all eleven ducklings were bobbing around like fluffy corks. The shelduck quacked a loud, grateful goodbye, and then they paddled out to sea.

Flotsam and Jetsam watched as the duck family vanished into the distance.

They looked at the whoosh. "Sainsbury could slide down that too," said Jetsam softly. "He'd like that."

"He would," agreed Flotsam.

But Sainsbury didn't feel like trying it just then. And when they all went into the boat house, it felt strangely empty.

"Us can eat indoors again, I suppose," murmured Flotsam. "That'll be good, now it's got so rainy, won't it?"

"It will," said Jetsam. "And us can sleep in our JA FA bed again. It will be nice and dry." She sighed. "I expect it shall need some new seaweed in it. That duck will have squashed it good and proper." She went to look inside their bed, and gasped. "Look! Flotsam! Come and see!"

When Flotsam saw what was inside their JA FA bed, he gasped too.

The crunchy, rough, dried seaweed that they used to sleep on was nowhere to be seen. The duck had covered it with the softest, downiest, deepest bed of feathers that Flotsam and Jetsam had ever seen.

Jetsam reached out to stroke them.

"'Twill be glorious warm," said Jetsam.

"'Twill be proper cosy," agreed Flotsam.

"Us shall be wondrous comfortable. Sure as soft pillows is soft pillows. Sure as fluffy blankets is fluffy blankets. 'Tis a proper marvellous present."

Feeling very happy, Flotsam and Jetsam tucked themselves into the downy warmth of their JA FA bed. Sainsbury curled up happily in the toe of his wellington boot. As they fell asleep, nothing stirred on their

little beach but the sea. Nothing disturbed
the silence but the gentle lapping of
the waves, and the rise and fall of soft,
contented breathing that drifted out of the
doorway of the boat house.

When the tide was high, the sea calm, and the moon bright enough to cast shadows, the old man and the young boy set out along the cliff path for some night fishing.

If they had paused for a moment and looked down, they would have seen a little beach with an upturned boat in the middle and a rainbow-striped umbrella beside it. They might have noticed a child's bicycle wheel lying flat, covered with a disc of lino, as if some small person had made themselves a roundabout. If they had looked really hard they might have noticed a sheet of plastic on the sloping sand with a well-worn groove down the middle as if someone had used it as a slide.

But they didn't look. They didn't even glance down. To them it was just a little beach, nestling at the bottom of high cliffs: impossible to get to on foot and not worth visiting by boat – too small to bother with.

Nobody has ever stopped. Nobody has ever looked down. The beach remains unnoticed and undisturbed, which is just as well.

It is the whole world to Flotsam and Jetsam and Sainsbury.

If you go to the seaside, try making your own
Flotsam and Jetsam figures on the sand. Be sure to
take a photo before the tide comes in!

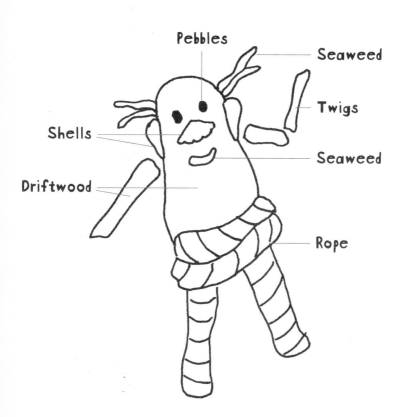

Pebbles

Seaweed

Twigs

Shells

Seaweed

Driftwood

Rope

Visit **www.tanyalandman.com** to send Tanya
your photos and hear more from Flotsam and Jetsam.

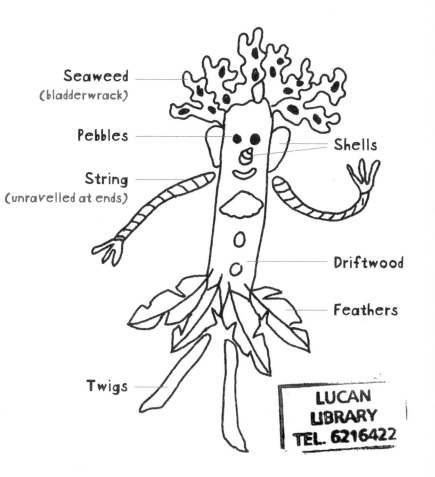

Seaweed
(bladderwrack)

Pebbles

String
(unravelled at ends)

Shells

Driftwood

Feathers

Twigs

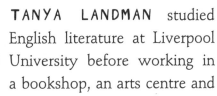

TANYA LANDMAN studied English literature at Liverpool University before working in a bookshop, an arts centre and a zoo. She is the author of many books for children, including *Merlin's Apprentice*, *Waking Merlin*, *The World's Bellybutton*, *The Kraken Snores*, *Mary's Penny* and the Sam Swann movie mysteries, and she won the Red House Children's Book Award for *Mondays are Murder*, the first of ten murder mysteries about the intrepid Poppy Fields. Since 1992, Tanya has also been a part of Storybox Theatre. She lives with her family in Devon.

RUTH RIVERS was brought up in the East Midlands and now lives in London. She almost dropped art aged fourteen as she wanted to be a vet – but luckily she was persuaded to continue and went on to study graphic design at Exeter College of Art and Design. She has illustrated a number of children's books, including *The Biggest Bible Storybook* by Anne Adeney and *Matty Mouse* by Jenny Nimmo.